For my good friend Paeony Lewis
DB

For Heidi, Chloe and Ben
for their love, support and cups of tea
DH

LITTLE TIGER PRESS
1 The Coda Centre, 189 Munster Road, London SW6 6AW
www.littletiger.co.uk
First published in Great Britain 2003
This edition published in the United States 2014

What Are You Doing in
My Bed?

by David Bedford
Illustrated by Daniel Howarth

LITTLE TIGER PRESS
London

Kip the kitten had nowhere to sleep
on a dark and cold winter's night.
So he crept through a door . . .

. . . and curled up warm and
snug in somebody's bed.

Then out of the dark,
Kip heard . . .

. . . whispers and hisses,
and soft feet padding
through the night.

Bright green eyes peered
in through the window,
and suddenly . . .

. . . one, two, three, four, five, six cats
came banging through the cat door!
They tumbled and skidded and rolled
across the floor, where they found . . .

. . . Kip!
"What are YOU doing in OUR bed?"
shouted the six angry cats.

"Your bed?" said Kip.
"But this bed's too small for
  you. You'd never all fit!"

"Never fit?" said the cats.
"Just you watch . . . ."

One, two, three cats curled up
neatly, head to tail . . .

then four, five, six cats
piled on top.

"See? There's no room
    for you," they said.
"You'd never fit."

"Never fit?"
    said Kip.
"Just you
    watch . . . ."

Tottering and teetering,
Kip carefully climbed on top.
 "I'll sleep here," he said.

"OK," the cats yawned.
"But don't fidget or snore."
 And they fell asleep in a heap.

But suddenly, a big, deep,
growly voice said . . .

"WHAT ARE YOU DOING IN MY BED? SCRAM!"

The cats scattered around the room, but they only found hard, cold places to sleep.

Harry the dog was comfy in his bed,
and he soon began to snore.

But then an icy wind whistled in
through the cat door, and Harry
awoke and shivered.

Kip whispered, "Follow me,"
and he quickly led six cold cats
across the floor . . .

. . . to the cozy bed.
"We'll keep you warm,"
said Kip.

"You'll never all fit," chattered Harry.
"Never fit?" said Kip. "Just you watch . . . ."

Kip and Harry snored right through the night under their warm blanket of cats.

And they all fit purr-fectly!